# The Way to the Zoo

For Sylvie, who always puts you through.

First published 2014 by Walker Books Ltd
87 Vauxhall Walk, London SE11 5HJ

10 9 8 7 6 5 4 3 2 1

The right of John Burningham to be identified as author/illustrator of this
work has been asserted by him in accordance with the Copyright, Designs
and Patents Act 1988

This book has been typeset in URW Egyptienne T

Printed in China

British Library Cataloguing in Publication Data:
a catalogue record for this book is available from
the British Library

ISBN 978-1-4063-4840-8

www.walker.co.uk

# The Way to the Zoo

## JOHN BURNINGHAM

WALKER BOOKS
AND SUBSIDIARIES
LONDON · BOSTON · SYDNEY · AUCKLAND

One evening, just before Sylvie went to sleep, she thought she could see a door in the wall of her bedroom.

Sylvie decided to look again in the morning to see if the door was really there.

In the morning, Sylvie was late for school
and forgot about the door until bedtime.

When Sylvie was ready for bed
she found the door and managed to open it.
She could see some steps going down,
and beyond there was a passage.

Sylvie found the torch and went down the steps and along the passage for a while, wondering where it would go to.

In the distance, she could see what seemed to be another door.

The door was very difficult to open,
but Sylvie used all her strength
and at last it opened.

Sylvie found herself in the zoo
with lots of animals looking at her.

It was getting late. Sylvie had to get back to her room and go to sleep because it was school again in the morning. Sylvie asked a little bear to come back with her and the bear slept in her bed.

She had to make sure the bear was back in the zoo and the door in her wall was closed before she went to school.

All the animals wanted to come to Sylvie's room,
but she could only take the smaller ones.

One night she brought the penguins back,

but they made a lot of mess splashing water in the bathroom.

Then she came back with a tiger and her cub.

The tiger slept in a chair and her cub
slept in Sylvie's bed.

Another night Sylvie let the birds come.

Sylvie had to ask some
animals to leave because
they stole things ...

or were too smelly to have in her room.

The baby elephant burst into tears
because it was too big for the passage.

A baby rhino was able to get through the passage.
Sylvie did not want the rhino in her bed
so she wrapped it up in towels for the night.

Sylvie had different animals
in her room every night.

One morning Sylvie woke up very late and had to rush to get ready for her mother to take her to school.

When she came home, she knew something was wrong.

There were noises coming from the sitting room.

She had forgotten to close the door in her bedroom wall.

The sitting room was full of animals.

Sylvie was very cross
and all the animals left.

Sylvie knew her mother would be back soon and she had very little time to clean and tidy the room.

Sylvie had only just finished when her mother arrived.

"Oh Sylvie, Sylvie," her mother said. "All I have to do is leave you while I am out for a while and it looks as if you had the whole zoo here!"

Sylvie still sometimes has animals to visit at night, perhaps a baby bear or something furry.

But she always makes sure the way to the zoo is closed before she goes to school.